Don't Go Into The Cellar, Mr Holmes!

Sherlock Holmes Stories Re-Imagined for the Stage

Jonathan Goodwin

Copyright

First edition published in 2021
© Copyright 2021 Jonathan Goodwin

The right of Jonathan Goodwin to be identified as the author of this work has been asserted by him in accordance with the Copyright, Designs and Patents Act 1998.

All rights reserved. No reproduction, copy or transmission of this publication may be made without express prior written permission. No paragraph of this publication may be reproduced, copied or transmitted except with express prior written permission or in accordance with the provisions of the Copyright Act 1956 (as amended). Any person who commits any unauthorised act in relation to this publication may be liable to criminal prosecution and civil claims for damage.

Although every effort has been made to ensure the accuracy of the information contained in this book, as of the date of publication,
nothing herein should be construed as giving advice. The opinions expressed herein are those of the author and not of MX Publishing.

Paperback ISBN 978-1-78705-895-8
AUK ePub 978-1-78705-896-5
AUK PDF 978-1-78705-897-2

Published by MX Publishing
335 Princess Park Manor, Royal Drive, London, N11 3GX
www.mxpublishing.co.uk

Cover design by Brian Belanger.

Photography by www.giacomogiannelli.com

Contents

Introduction	3
Theatre in pictures	7
The Adventure Of The Medium	11
Holmes Alone	28
Sherlock Holmes and The Mazarin Malediction	63
The Giant Rat of Sumatra	87
The Adventure of The Amazonian Explorer	106

To my wonderful wife Siân, *The* Woman in my life, I dedicate this book.

Introduction

This book is well overdue. I should have written it years ago, but it's ironically the current pandemic that has brought it to fruition. The pandemic that has robbed us of live audiences for far too long opened another door – the online performance. Whilst nothing can replace the exhilaration of the live audience sitting a few metres away from you, performing online has brought our performances to an entirely new fan base – a global one.

This book contains five scripts, three of which I owe a great debt of gratitude to Tony Reynolds as they are taken from his wonderful book of Sherlock Holmes stories 'The Lost Stories of Sherlock Holmes'. As for the others, "Holmes Alone" is a light-hearted romp, that borrows elements and characters from several other Conan Doyle tales. "The Mazarin Malediction" is my attempt to embellish that oft-maligned story, "The Mazarin Stone". Almost always it's this story in particular that is singled out for harsh criticism. Yet I have always enjoyed the tale, and the others in the collection entitled "The Case-Book of Sherlock Holmes". "Malediction" is my homage to ACD's original, written and performed with great affection and enjoyment.

A massive thanks to the wonderful Jeremy Brett whose memory I am saluting with these performances. I first 'played' Brett early in 2021 in A Tribute to Jeremy Brett and got such a wonderful reaction that I continued with these stories. I genuinely hope that I am given the opportunity to bring Jeremy back to the stage again one day.

I hope you have the chance to see us perform *live-live*, or *online-live*, or peruse our many recordings on our brand spanking new online shop!

To all the Sherlock fans out there, may our performances continue to be 'Strictly Sherlock' and bring a smile to your lips. My especial thanks to Gary Archer, with whom I run Don't Go Into The Cellar! And to Sian, who has since lockdown started, become my de facto sound-and-camera woman. Little could she have known when she said "I do" that her duties would soon involve theatre stage management. It really does pay to read the small print, you know.

Jonathan Goodwin, September 2021

Theatre in Pictures

The Adventure of the Medium

I was becoming a little stale being in the metropolis. A change of scene in a strange town may be exactly what was required. According to the letter I had received that morning, the client lived in Birmingham. A visit ought to be sufficient to interrupt the even yet uneventful tenor of my life, and that of friend Watson also.

The letter read as follows.

Sir,

While the intrusion of outsiders into family matters is deeply distasteful to me, nevertheless I believe your skill in detecting impostors and charlatans may be valuable.

I would ask you to present yourself at my offices on the 21st of this month. I will give you full details. You will find your remuneration paid at the most generous scale.

Yours faithfully,
JAMES MURCHISON

Watson informed me that Murchison's Haberdashery happened to be a large manufacturing concern. I noted how the pen had dug deeper at the words *impostors* and *charlatans*. This no doubt accounts for his rather peremptory tone. On consideration I believe I will go to Birmingham, after all.

Watson and I set off the following day. A journey of somewhat more than two hours took us to Birmingham New Street station. From there we took a hansom cab to the premises of Murchison Haberdashery. We gave our names to the porter, and we were shown to Murchison's rather palatial office. He rose to greet us.

HOLMES becomes MURCHISON

Ah, Mr. Holmes, I am delighted to meet you. And you as well, of course, Dr Watson. If you will be seated, I will outline the problem.

I wish you, Mr. Holmes, to expose a fraudster. Of a rather unusual kind. It is also, I have to say, a matter most embarrassing to me. It is essential that no word of this be generally known. You see, it is not I, but my wife who is being most cruelly deceived. You should know that we lost our son, our only child, in the Transvaal war a few years ago. My wife was inconsolable, as you will appreciate. And then she fell into the power of a woman who calls herself a medium. Madame Beverley claims to be in touch with the spirit of our boy.

My wife is completely under the spell of this woman. She talks of nothing but the séances she attends and the messages that purportedly come from our child.

There is also the question of money. This medium charges for her services. A lot of money has already been paid to her. I believe the greater part of my wife's allowance for each month goes to this woman. As this charlatan is properly housed, an action cannot be brought against her under the Vagrancy Act. Essentially, unless the medium predicts misfortune it is not illegal to practice. She has been careful in fact to predict nothing at all. She claims to be merely a conduit for the voice of our son. But I was hoping that with your noted skills you might be able to see a way through, Mr Holmes.

Reverts to HOLMES

This was certainly an unusual case. A wrongdoer committing a fraud that is based on the supernatural. The normal rules of evidence therefore would not apply. It would be impossible to prove that these messages were not genuine. But if the medium used some of the characteristic tricks of her trade, then perhaps fraud could be demonstrated to my client's wife.

Clearly, I needed to interview Mrs Murchison. Friend Watson and I would introduce ourselves as members of the Psychical Research Society of King's College. We would say that we had heard glowing reports of Madame Beverley and wished to talk to one that knows her. Then I shall ask to be introduced and to attend a séance.

Murchison would arrange to have bogus visiting cards engraved for our use. Also he recommended an hotel whereat we could stay for the duration of this investigation. That evening, I discussed things as they stood with Watson.

We would need to be our guard at the séance. Firstly, the room will be darkened to conceal as far as possible the medium's actions. Mediums almost always work at their own homes, for obvious reasons. Objects and apparatus can be concealed before the clients arrive. An accomplice can be hidden behind a screen or curtains, to make sounds, shine lights. The medium may also have apparatus concealed about her person. There are a thousand tricks, and I hope to see some ingenious variants of them.

Watson was prepared to give some of them the benefit of the doubt, of course. He cited one Helen Berry, who allegedly formed a small child from ectoplasm in the presence of witnesses. I suggested some gauzy fabric covered with fluorescent paint. An accomplice and some imagination would do the rest.

There was nothing supernatural in this. Rather, it had all to do with the basic human emotions of grief and greed. The strong need of a bereaved mother to be comforted. The lust for money in the wicked person who plays upon this sorrow.

The next morning, we ordered a cab and rattled through the streets of Birmingham to Murchison's mansion in Edgbaston. We gave in our cards at the door and were conducted to the drawing room. There we were greeted by our client and his wife.

Mrs Murchison, we are here in connection with Madame Beverley. Remarkable stories of her powers have reached our Society. We have been despatched to look into the matter further. Can you first tell me when you first made the acquaintance of this lady? About four months ago, you say. And how did it happen that you met her?

Mrs Murchison said Madame Beverly had written to her at that address. She said that the dead Murchison boy had communicated with her during a séance. It was common knowledge that the son had been killed in the South African campaign. His mother believed the letter to be a vulgar attempt to coerce her into attending her séances. But then her letter went on to say that to the last he remembered my quoting, *Where there is fear, there cannot be wisdom. This was a favourite quotation of Mrs Murchison, something only the son could have known about. And so she had attended the séance the next day. A*t that séance her son spoke to her, she claimed.

The voice was that of Tom? She accepted that it had changed somewhat, being rather hoarser than in life and a little slurred. But all the turns of phrase were his, and he spoke of incidents from his childhood that could not have been known by any other. It had not been Madame Beverley's either, for it was much lower than a woman could produce.

I asked to see a photograph of the deceased. It showed Tom just before he had left for the Transvaal. He wore the uniform of the 58th Regiment of Foot, the Rutlandshires.

Mrs. Murchison said her family had service connections with the regiment. At that point, the husband interjected.

HOLMES as MURCHISON

The 58th is one of our hardiest regiments, Mr. Holmes. The men are nick-named the Steel-Backs because of their complete indifference to floggings. We were glad to see him do his duty for Queen and country. It was also, I believed, advantageous for him to find an outlet for his youthful energy. In a few years of course, I would have hoped that he would come back to England and settle down to learning the business and take over the running of it from me. But this was never meant to be. He was sent with his regiment to put down the Transvaal rebellion and killed in action at the battle of Majuba Hill. That would have been three years ago.

Reverts to HOLMES

Mrs. Murchison told us how the enemy had advanced under cover and shot very accurately. Though the order was given to retreat, the Boers had gained the summit and it soon became a rout. Thomas had been shot in the head and died instantly. That was according to Madame Beverley, of course. She had said the spirit of Tom was communicating through her. A very circumstantial account which possessed the stamp of veracity.

I asked Mrs. Murchison if Watson and I could attend a séance and afterwards talk to Madame Beverley. It was arranged for that evening. Indeed, Mrs. Murchison was Madame Beverley's only client. Unusual! Mrs. Murchison explained she gave Madame Beverley enough to live on, a stipend as it were. With that, Watson and I took our leave.

There was no question that someone who knew Thomas Murchison well was involved. A servant, for example, would be familiar with his history and his manner of speech. That evening we sallied from our hotel and hired a hansom to take us to Handsworth, a respectable working-class neighbourhood.

We climbed the steps to the entrance and rang the bell. The door was opened by a small, rotund lady in a purple dress. This excitable woman introduced herself as Mrs. Barnard, the next-door neighbour. She led us a few steps down the hall and into a small parlour. The space in the room was largely taken up by a large, circular mahogany table. Dining chairs had been placed around it. Mrs.

Murchison was already present and talking to a slightly-built young woman. This was Madame Beverley.

What a pleasure to make your acquaintance! You are truly gifted if what I hear is correct. I am honoured to attend this evening. There are still many who will not open their minds to the infinite.

The lights were lowered. I requested that Watson be permitted to sit near one of the undimmed lamps, as he was to take notes. Madame Beverley took her place in the large, winged chair, with Mrs. Murchison and I seated either side of her.

The medium leaned back in her chair with her eyes closed. She called on the dead man, Thomas, to make his presence known. Abruptly, her face slackened. Her breathing became stertorous. When she spoke, the voice was certainly not her own. It was much lower and hoarser in tone and seemed somehow hollow.

Mother! Mother, you must not grieve. I have gone where we all must go. Soon enough we will be together. I cannot stay. Be happy, mother.

There was silence for a time, then the medium stirred and came to her senses. Mrs Murchison was evidently pleased with the results of the séance. Madame Beverley asked Watson and me to leave, owing to her extreme weariness.

Mrs. Murchison offered us a lift in her carriage, but I declined. Watson and I discussed what we had seen as we walked. Naturally, he had been impressed by the young woman, owing to her physical appearance. But she was plainly an actress. At least she had convincingly imitated sincerity. The cosmetics she wore had been expertly applied in the manner used in the acting profession. Rather bold strokes and more emphatic colouring so that the effect is best seen from beyond the footlights.

And then Watson surprised me, by remarking that he had noticed Madame Beverley was with child. The raised colour in her cheeks, the slight thickening about her waist, swollen ankles. Unmistakeable tell-tale signs. He estimated she was in her fourth or fifth month.

Therefore through Watson's acute observation, we could conclude that a man was involved.

Watson and I wended our way through some narrow and dirty streets to the premises of *Jasper Ellis, File & Rasp Manufacturer*. I had placed an order with Mr Ellis that afternoon. True to his word, the work had been completed. Upon receipt of payment, he handed me a small parcel done up in brown paper. We summoned a cab and retired to our hotel, but only for a few hours. I told Watson we were to return to Madame Beverley's residence before daybreak, and not in an altogether law-abiding capacity.

In the early hours of the morning, we walked the mile or so back to Handsworth. Outside the house, I made sure we were unobserved. I led the way down the steps to the area. There I opened my Gladstone bag and produced the tool given to me by Ellis. It was a slim steel rod mounted on a stout wooden handle. With this I was able to force the lock to the sash, and so gain entry to the property.

I shone my dark lantern around the room. There were pieces of sewing and other domestic paraphernalia. Above us, I saw what I was looking for. It was a speaking tube! Evidently the accomplice would be stationed by that tube. It runs up inside the medium's chair and terminates in one of the chair wings. By putting it to his ear, the events of the séance can be overheard clearly. He would also speak into the tube. His voice would apparently be emanating from the mouth of the medium. A simple but effective trick.

We searched the room for papers or other belongings that might shed further light on the identity of this other person. We could not go to the upper floors as the risk of detection would be too great. Finally we put everything back where we had found it and left the house by the area door. At least we had proof that Madame Beverley was a fraud. But I doubted this would be enough to destroy Mrs Murchison's faith. There remained a person with an intimate knowledge of Tom's life, prepared to betray his memory for money. I owed it to my client to find that person and to expose him.

I awoke later than usual that morning, to find that Watson had gone out. When he returned, he was in exuberant spirits. He had solved the case, or so he claimed.

Watson told me had had visited a public-house, *The Black Eagle,* in Handsworth where old soldiers would meet. There the landlord had told Watson one of the regulars had been injured at Majuba Hill. Evidently this man must have been a comrade of Tom Murchison. He would have been privy to all the small details of Tom's life. After being discharged as wounded, he returned to his native town. Here he took up with the woman, Madame Beverley.

Between them they hit on the perfect way of making money. She would purport to be in contact with the spirit of the dead. He cannot imitate Tom's voice, so he simply speaks hoarsely. This would also explain why she concealed his existence.

I asked Watson if he knew the nature of the fraudster's injuries. Ah! He had been hit by a rifle bullet in the jaw. That may be significant.

A short while later we knocked on the medium's door. She opened it herself. She allowed us inside, albeit grudgingly. The room in which the séance had happened looked shabbier in the daylight. Madame Beverley shut the door and joined us.

Before I began, I asked that her gentleman companion join us also. What I had to say concerned him as much as it did her. However, she refused. Very well then. I would appeal to her as a woman soon to become a mother herself, to consider the feelings of another mother who has lost her child. Mrs Murchison's grief for her son brought her much suffering. Madame Beverley however was aware that Thomas Murchison was still alive. I wished her to confess as much to the young man's parents. If she did not, then I would tell the truth of the matter.

Madame Beverley said nothing. I heard footsteps ascending the stairs from the basement. The door opened and a young man walked in. The lower part of his face was muffled in a scarf. He took her by the hand.

HOLMES as THOMAS MURCHISON

I was listening at the speaking tube. Please be seated gentlemen. You are correct, Mr Holmes, in deducing that I am Thomas Murchison. From the moment we landed in Africa we were fighting an enemy we did not know how to deal with. We suffered a continuous loss of men. We were marched into the Drakensberg mountains. We were ordered to encamp on Majuba Hill. The Boers attacked us later that day. You could barely see the enemy, the smoke from their rifles was so thick.

In truth it was more that we ran for our lives than retreated. In the scramble I was wounded in the face. The bullet entered behind my left ear and shattered my jaw as it exited. I rolled the rest of the way down the slope and lay unconscious for a time. When I came to myself it was almost dark. I crawled away. Eventually I had the good fortune to fall in with an old hunter of English extraction. He bound up my wounds and stayed with me until I was strong enough to walk. Then he gave me a few supplies and left me.

I made my way to the coast at Durban. The journey took over a year, and I had to beg my bread. In the first week of my travels a farmer's wife gave me some cast-off clothes. I no longer had to wear the tatters of my uniform.

Finally I arrived back at my hometown. I could not bring myself to contact my parents. How could I? My mother had always been so proud of my handsome looks. My father would despise a man who had run away from the enemy and then deserted his regiment. I preferred that they believed that I died fighting for my country.

Instead, I contacted my darling Jenny. We came to love one another, but I could not tell my parents of this. They would not consider an actress suitable for their only son. Jenny took me in and cared for me. Shortly afterwards we married.

I cannot find employment. My appearance disgusts people. I cannot even draw a soldier's pension as I deserted the colours. We were forced to depend on Jenny's *earnings on the stage. When she realised that she was to become a mother, we faced starvation, not only for ourselves but for our child.*

It was then that we struck on the idea of approaching my mother with a tale of communicating with my spirit. It was wrong, I know. But after all, it was my own family from which I was taking money. We aimed at getting enough money to emigrate to one of the colonies. I could become a farmer. My appearance would not matter. Over there, a man's worth is not measured by his looks.

There was no need to continue with this deception. I was convinced his parents would forgive him and welcome his wife. Watson and I would accompany them when he broke the news to them. A four-wheeler conveyed the four of us to the Murchison home. When we came into their presence, they looked in shock and disbelief at the ravaged face of their son. Then Mrs. Murchison ran towards him and embraced him. The father grasped Thomas's hand. The news that they would soon be grandparents made their happiness complete.

As Watson and I made to leave, Mr. Murchison asked us to step into his study. There he produced his check-book and proceeded to write rapidly.

As MURCHISON

There Mr. Holmes, I hope you will consider this adequate compensation for your labours. It is small recompense indeed for all you have done.

Reverts to HOLMES

And so we took our leave.

Always remember that although it was very unlikely, it was not impossible that Thomas might have deserted his regiment or been captured and imprisoned by the enemy. Watson's discovery of a local man who was at Majuba Hill was invaluable. For this person to be a close friend of Thomas, and also resident in Birmingham was too much. The injury to his jaw gave a clear explanation of the change in voice. The fact that Madame Beverley took money from Mrs Murchison alone made the matter clear.

Holmes Alone

SFX Voiceover, DR WATSON

The first years of the twentieth-century marked a time of change in the British Empire. As the Victorian era ended with the sad passing of Her Majesty, so King Edward's reign ushered in a brave new world of social and political upheaval. Yet crime and its practitioners remained the same, thereby allowing my friend Mr Sherlock Holmes ample opportunity to exercise those peculiar gifts for which he has become world-renowned.

But time stands still for no one, whether he be the world's first and foremost consulting detective, or his faithful biographer. Following my late wife Mary's unhappy passing I feared I would see out the remainder of my days alone, a relic of the Victorian past. But destiny had a surprise in store for me when I chanced to encounter the delightful Alice, who made even a confirmed widower such as I the happiest man in England by consenting to become my bride.

Married life meant that I saw less and less of Holmes. Although he still had his chemical experiments, his violin, his good old Index and of course the not infrequent cries for assistance from Lestrade and Gregson to occupy his energies, by 1904 Holmes had finally tired of London and its myriad distractions and decided to retire. And yet, even in retirement, and some years beyond Baker Street, the tentacles of crime could still reach as far as the South Downs.

As I trawl through my case-notes, the news-clippings and reports of the years gone by restore the ghosts of the past. I am reminded of the eccentric naturalist, Joyce-Armstrong, whose beach-combing uncovered a spate of inexplicable deaths along the coastline, including that of Myrtle, the promising young aeronaut whose head remains missing even to this day. I can still recall with a thrill the terror and mystification that gripped London following the theft of the fabulous Blue Carbuncle and of the fear with which Britons read of the crime spree being committed by the brutish malefactor known only as The Hoxton Creeper! Indeed, little could I have known at the time that I was soon to become embroiled in the same tangled skein and that at the behest of Mr Mycroft Holmes himself, that enigmatic and quite brilliant servant of His Majesty's Government, his younger brother Sherlock was to be brought out of retirement to investigate!

It was the year 1913. War clouds were looming over Europe, but little could Holmes have envisaged the singular sequence of events that were soon to engage the amazing powers of him whom I shall ever regard as the best and wisest man I have ever known.

Enter SHERLOCK HOLMES

Ah! Welcome, my merry band of Irregulars, to this – my retreat upon the South Downs. Here, in the company of none save my redoubtable house-keeper, Mrs Turner, I am finally rid of the grime of that fascinating, debilitating, irresistible metropolis that for so many years was my home. London! That great cesspool into which all the thieves, forgers and murderers of the British Empire are irresistibly drained!

Whereas once I assiduously scrutinised the patterns of behaviour amongst the criminal element of the City, now I study my beloved bees. Indeed, though my career as a consulting detective has drawn to a close, I have not been idle during my retirement, oh no! For my work upon my grand magnum opus, *The Practical Handbook of Bee Culture, with Some Observation upon the Segregation of the Queen*, is almost complete!

Save for Mrs Turner, I see little enough of other people these days. My good friend, Watson, visits me occasionally, but has recently taken a new bride – his second, or is it his third? The Doctor always did have an appreciation of the gentler sex. Therefore, I see even less of him now than I did before; but this is an isolated act of selfishness on his part, and one which I can easily forgive. As for myself, I have always maintained that women are never to be trusted – not even the best of them! Why, the most charming woman I ever encountered poisoned three small children, and as for Irene Adler - !

No, my dear Irregulars, I am quite content here in Sussex. My otherwise-idyllic existence is intermittently interrupted, however, by an amateur astronomer who lives in the nearby village of Fulworth. Mr Joyce-Armstrong's latest *idee-fixe* proved to be so overwhelming, that it brought him to my cottage one bright spring morning. The staccato knock upon the front door was sufficient to dampen my spirits, knowing as I did that my studies with the bees were curtailed for as long as it took for my neighbour to unburden himself of his latest wildest theories.

HOLMES becomes JOYCE-ARMSTRONG

You must forgive this sudden intrusion, Mr Holmes! But I simply *had* to inform you of my latest discoveries, for who knows *what* precisely they may portend?

You've seen the headlines recently in the local newspaper, Mr Holmes? You must have heard tell of the strange business involving the young aeronaut, whose body they found down by the shore? *Horribly mangled*, it was – or at least, the bits that were left were mangled, for *the head was missing!*

Oh, I know what you are thinking, Mr Holmes! Surely the coroner's court would have thought there was something remiss about the corpse being minus its noggin! Do you know, it was their opinion that the sheer force of the plummet from the heights drove his head clean through his torso?

Utter poppycock, I say!

Oh, I know what the papers say, Mr Holmes – that Lieutenant Myrtle pushed himself too far in trying to smash the height record, and that at 30, 000 feet he simply lost control of his aeroplane and spiralled to his doom. Ah! But I have seen things through my field glasses that would make your pipe curl, sir, even more so than it already has!

No, please let me finish, Mr Holmes, for I shan't take up too much of your time, and it is *vital* that this be brought to your attention! You may be aware that I am an amateur astronomer of some celebrity hereabouts, and that it's a rare evening indeed when I am not scouring the skies for constellations. But lately I have seen such wonders as to stagger the senses and boggle the mind!

That poor unfortunate, Lieutenant Myrtle, wasn't the only one whose death has had a shade of mystery attached to it, sir. You may have read of another young aeronaut, Mr Hay Connor, whose aeroplane came down close to Lower Haycock late last year. Oh! They found his aeroplane all right, but as for Hay Connor himself, naught but his old briar pipe that was last seen clenched between his teeth shortly before he took to the skies!

These were not ordinary deaths, Mr Holmes, but extraordinary *murders!* No, no! Please bear with me and allow me to explain my findings, sir.

I have been scanning the skies and have observed some very queer things indeed occurring high above us. My attention was first arrested one starlit night late last year. I was gazing at the stars through my lens, Mr Holmes. It must have been close to midnight, and the sky was clear, with each star shining like so many pinpricks of silvery light. It was then that I saw *the ooze* for the first time, Mr Holmes! It was like a great wave of gossamer silk, sir, streaming through the heavens.

I began to scrutinise the sky high above us, for such a sight was utterly unique to me. And the longer that I watched, and the closer that I studied, the more my disbelieving eyes witnessed!

They are horrors, Mr Holmes – horrors of the heights! I've seen 'em – snake-like creatures streaking athwart the skies, translucent and vaporous! Sometimes, on clear nights, I've been able to follow their serpentine trail twisting in and around the constellations! It looks like cloud cover, but I know better than that, Mr Holmes!

Yet worse than these, sir, are those other – *creatures!* Gigantic airborne monsters, vicious and viscous, with awesome domed bodies larger than St Paul's Cathedral, and wicked beaks snapping in-between their inky-black, deathly eyes.

And Mr Holmes, as for their tentacles, trailing after them in the stratosphere as they haul their monstrous torsos across the heavens – why, 'tis like something from the Old Testament, sir!

Just as there are dangerous and wild tracts of jungle here on earth, in Brazil and on the African continent, I maintain that there are similar regions miles above our heads also, riddled with creatures even more terrifying and deadlier than the most ferocious beasts on our planet. And it was the exploration of such strange and mysterious realms that drew poor Myrtle and Hay Connor to their gruesome deaths, Mr Holmes.

You must believe what I am telling you, because the authorities and the British Government won't listen to me, you see. They dismiss me as being a crank and an old fool, but if you went to them and told them what I have just told you, then they would be willing to do something about it. I've read of your exploits in *Strand Magazine,* and I know your brother Mr Mycroft Holmes has friends in high places.

But it's what lies in *these* high places that must be stopped, Mr Holmes! Innocent young lives have already been lost *up there*, but what should happen if those *things* up in the sky ever decided to descend to *terra firma*? Just think of the loss of life, sir!

Goodness me, there's someone at your front door, Mr Holmes – yes, 'tis the post-man, with a telegram for you by the looks of things.

Why, whatever is the matter, sir? You look as though you've seen a ghost. Well, if you absolutely insist that I leave right this minute – I was never one to outstay my welcome, you know. What, you're heading to London, Mr Holmes – unexpected emergency, you say? Well, really!

SFX Voiceover, DR WATSON

The Mazarin Stone had a purported street value close to one hundred thousand pounds, and yet in truth, its history and reputation rendered it priceless. Every facet stood for a bloody deed committed during its murky past. Already there had been two murders, a vitriol-throwing, a suicide and several robberies committed by those desperate to possess it. In its desperation to acquire the Stone, the British Government had already enlisted the services of two gentlemen from the wrong side of the law, and yet gentleman law-breaker and amateur cracksman alike had failed in their attempts.

And so it was on that bleak and blustery morning of 1913, that Sherlock Holmes once more was ensconced within

his familiar drawing-room of 221B Baker Street, playing host to that crabbed and venerable peer, Lord Cantlemere.

JOYCE-ARMSTRONG becomes LORD CANTLEMERE

Good morning, Mr Holmes. I must inform you that it is only at the behest of your brother, Mycroft that I am here to see you. I have never been entirely convinced by your unorthodox methods, sir, and have always been a staunch believer in our own Metropolitan police-force. Why rely on the theories of *amateurs*, Mr Holmes, when we already have professionals at our disposal?

However, I am forced to concede that your surmises were of some small consequence in bringing to a successful conclusion that rather unfortunate affair concerning the Duke of Holderness. And Mycroft Holmes assures me that despite your *eccentricities*, you are not without merit.

Mycroft undoubtedly informed you in his telegram of the news we have received concerning your erstwhile colleague, Doctor Watson, else I am certain you would not be here. He has been kidnapped and held to ransom, Mr Holmes, the ransom being the Mazarin Stone.

Tell me, Mr Holmes, what do you know of the Mazarin Stone? Ah! Such talk of the supernatural is nothing but arrant balderdash, sir, and nothing more! Why, if these tales were to be given credence, the Stone has driven men insane and impelled several to commit acts of self-destruction. It is all in the mind, Mr Holmes! Nevertheless, certain facts have come to light that convince us the safety of Great Britain will be compromised unless we recover the Stone post-haste.

Agents upon either side of the English Channel have already been deployed to retrieve the Stone, without success. Our very own A. J. Raffles is currently in Charing Cross Hospital in a critical condition, while the body of Arsene Lupin was found floating in the Seine last night. Although it is true that neither man adhered to the law, the loss of life is still regrettable.

The Government has received a communication from an unknown source, though we believe him to be a German agent. Either the Mazarin Stone is recovered and delivered into his hands within the next forty-eight hours, or a series of explosions will be triggered across the United Kingdom.

These *dynamiters* have added an extra incentive for you to cooperate, Mr Holmes. Doctor Watson is being held hostage at an unspecified location within the Limehouse region.

Unless you successfully recover this Mazarin Stone and deliver it into the hands of the enemy agent, within the next forty-eight hours, then the life of your friend Watson will be terminated.

SFX Voiceover, DR WATSON:

Count Negretto Sylvius, of 136 Moorside Gardens, London, was a devil incarnate. He was a famous game-shot, sportsman and man-about-town, and a despicable cad of the first water. Many a society lady had cause to regret the day she had ever caught sight of the swarthy fellow, for Count Sylvius was a lady-killer, a corrupter of ladies' honest souls and despoiler of all that was fine about the gentler sex. The late and unlamented Professor James Moriarty, that Napoleon of Crime and manipulator of nearly half that was evil and almost all that went undetected in London's criminal underworld, had been Count Sylvius's master, and on any number of occasions the Italian marksman had proven himself to be an invaluable member of Moriarty's gang. Now, however, the Mazarin Stone had come into the possession of this shark-like predator, and it was the task of Sherlock Holmes to recover the jewel in order to effect my safe deliverance!

CANTLEMERE becomes **COUNT NEGRETTO SYLVIUS**

(Throughout, the actor may select an audience member in the front row to serve as **HOLMES, SAM MERTON, et al)**

So here we are, finally in the private residence of the *great* Mr Sherlock Holmes! But do not worry, my friend – not even he can possibly know the whereabouts of the Mazarin Stone.

But wait! There is someone behind this curtain in the bay-window. Hist! There, slumped in that armchair! Why yes, it is – it is Holmes himself, and he is asleep! Stand guard at the door, Sam, lest the landlady should interrupt! This is too good an opportunity to miss, equipped as I am with my *sturdiest* walking-cane. Mr Holmes always had a wonderful brain, and any second now it shall be smashed and smeared across the floor for all to see!

The COUNT raises his cane to strike

Great God – it is only a wax bust!

The COUNT is startled by the sudden appearance of SHERLOCK HOLMES

Mr Holmes, it is you! What is that you say – Tavernier is as good at waxworks as Straubenzee is at airguns? I don't know what you mean, sir!

This waxwork *thing* was designed to give me a spot of target practice! Nonsense, Mr Holmes! Do I look like the kind of man who would fire an airgun from the window of the empty house opposite in hopes of blowing your brains out? I cannot deny that I meant to *knock* a little sense into you just now – and it is with good reason! You have provoked me, sir, by setting your minions, your agents on my tracks! First there was that old sporting man, and then this afternoon, the elderly lady in the Minories.

What's that you say? You thank me for picking up your parasol after you had dropped it? *Then it was YOU!* Bah! What the law has gained, the stage has surely lost, Mr Holmes. You are a man of exceptional talents; it would be a shame should any harm befall you.

You wish me to hand over the Mazarin Stone, Mr Holmes? Ha! Did you hear that, Sam? The detective here thinks that *I* have the missing diamond! How the devil should I know where it is, sir? What's that, Mr Holmes – I am absolute plate glass, and you can see right through to the back of my mind? Well then, you can see where the diamond is for yourself, in that case.

Ah! I admit nothing, sir! What is in that little black book you have there? What – every detail of my vile and dangerous life? Ha! That would make for interesting reading indeed!

The deaths of Miss Minnie Warrender and young Arbothnot; the Riviera robbery; the forged cheque on the

Credit Lyonnais – no, you are wrong about the forged cheque!

No, Holmes – that does *not* mean you were right about all of the others. Eh, Mr Holmes? So you say you have evidence to prove that I have the Stone – the Whitehall cabman, the commissionaire, and – and *Ikey Sanders!* You *know* that he refused to cut up the diamond for me – damn!

Do you hear that, Sam? Mr Holmes wants me to reveal the whereabouts of the Mazarin Stone, else you and I are going to jail! I shan't tell you, Mr Holmes – *damn it all*!

What's that, Holmes – why yes, we do wish to be left alone for a few moments! You go into your bedroom and play your blasted violin!

SFX, *violin music*

What is to be done, Sam? Curse that fool of a coward, Ikey Sanders! I have to get the Stone out of the country at all costs. Bah! How can I be expected to think clearly with that blasted fiddle scratching at my ears?!

Wait – did you hear something, Sam? No, it must have been my imagination – that dreadful waxwork has unsettled my nerves. No, let me think, Sam…

SYLVIUS takes the Stone from his pocket and holds it aloft

I have the Stone in my pocket, and it can be out of England tonight. It will be in Amsterdam and cut it into four pieces before Saturday. There is not a moment to lose, Sam! One of us must take the stone to Van Seddor immediately. We can fool Holmes easily enough. We'll put him on the wrong track, and before he knows it, the Mazarin Stone shall be in Amsterdam, and we shall be out of the country!

Reverts to HOLMES

Thank you very much, Count! It was a simple case of substitution, ladies and gentlemen. I switched places with the waxwork behind the curtain and was thereby able to listen to their rather racy conversation.

Ah yes, ladies and gentlemen, the sound of my violin! Those modern gramophones are a wonderful invention!

Gregson, take them away!

With the Mazarin Stone at last in my possession, I sped to the Diogenes Club, where brother Mycroft and Lord Cantlemere both awaited my presence. The jewel had been placed within the wall-safe, and we were discussing what our next steps were to be, when a terrible din from the hallway alerted us to some new danger.

Mycroft – it's the *Hoxton Creeper!* It seems that in addition to snapping the backs of his victims, he has added theft to his *modus operandi.* Hullo – he's making towards the wall-safe!

Creeper – keep away from there! No, it's too late, Mycroft – he's actually wrenching the door of the safe off its hinges! The Creeper's strength is unbelievable. And – and yes, he's got the Mazarin Stone!

Stay where you are - *whatever* you are – it's the Mazarin Stone we want, and not you. Return the diamond to us immediately, and you can walk free.

Hullo – he's charging towards the window.

Creeper – don't do it, man! We're on the fourth floor – you won't survive the fall!

He's flung himself through the plate-glass window – why, surely not even The Creeper could have survived that. But look, gentlemen – there's not a sign of him anywhere, only shards of broken glass.

Anomalies of nature standing six foot nine inches tall do not simply disappear into thin air, however. Therefore, if he is not down there, then he has to be *up there*...

Do you see, Mycroft – do you see it? There's *The Creeper*, clinging to a rope-ladder suspended from a Zeppelin dirigible! Clearly then much preparation and planning went into the execution of this crime.

HOLMES *holds aloft a gramophone recording from a* ***man-servant***

Why, you say this recording has been delivered, with instructions for us to play it? Mycroft, have you a gramophone here at The Diogenes?

SFX, sound of crackling gramophone

HOLMES becomes VON BORK

Congratulations, Herr Holmes, and I salute your ingenuity in recovering the Mazarin Stone for me! By now I expect you will have made the acquaintance of *The Creeper*. I find him extremely useful, and what he lacks in sophistication, he more than compensates for in directness.

I imagine you want me now to release your friend, the Doctor, since you have complied with my demands and handed the Mazarin Stone over to me. Alas, Herr Holmes, I am a German and so the outdated British notion of *fair play* is completely alien to me.

Doctor Watson remains entrapped within the abandoned warehouse of the ship-builders *Ormond Sacker & Sons* in Limehouse. There you will find him in something of an awkward position. He is secured to a bench above which is descending a razor-sharp pendulum. With each passing moment the blade drops another fraction, until slicing the Doctor in two! Unless, that is, you release him.

However, Herr Holmes, should Doctor Watson be freed, the sudden decrease in weight upon the bench will set in motion a mechanism that triggers a trebuchet! Upon this trebuchet is a projectile containing the plague bacillus, Herr Holmes! Henceforth, it will be sent soaring through the sky-light into the waiting waters of the River Thames nearby. The plague will be disseminated in the water supply and – well, you know the rest.

Herr Holmes! You have a choice – either you will spare your beloved Watson and consign the people of London to a terrible death, *or* the City will be spared but the Doctor dies!

Choose wisely, detective! Doctor Watson has not got all night, you know! *Toodle pip,* Herr Holmes!

Reverts to HOLMES

Mycroft, Lord Cantlemere – you remain here, whilst I summon Wiggins and the Irregulars. There is not a moment to lose!

HOLMES becomes WIGGINS

In answer to the summons, me and the other Irregulars assembled and awaited Mr Holmes's instructions. He instructed Billy and the others to keep an eye out for the airship, and to report back as to the course it was taking. As for me, I was to make haste to the dockyards and find old Mordecai Smith, who owned a launch named the *Aurora*. He owed Mr Holmes a favour or two, and now it was time for him to cough up!

Mr Smith was to steer his launch down the Thames to a certain spot just within sight of Ormond Sacker & Sons and await further instructions. Oh, and I was to ask Mr Smith if his business was insured against fire.

Here, I can't 'ang around 'ere all night, you lot – I've got important work on my plate! Got to catch up with Billy and see what news him and the others have regarding that airship. Ta-rah!

SFX, swinging pendulum

WIGGINS becomes DR WATSON – his arms are outstretched, and he stands upright – the effect is that the audience is espying WATSON from above

Oh I say, old man, what a bloody relief it is to see you here! I'd said goodbye to Mary and was on my way to the surgery when some damned blackguard knocked me on the back of the head. And when to my senses I came, I found I was strapped to this workbench waiting to be sliced in two by that ruddy great blade hanging above.

Be a good chap, Holmes, and untie me, won't you? Yes, yes, I know all about the plague bacillus, but I can't very well be of much assistance like this. You'll find a way, Holmes, as always you do – but *after* you've freed me, what? Besides, London has faced the plague before and is here still, so I shouldn't worry too much.

What's that you say, old boy - my war wound? Why, my knee is the least of my worries right now! Have I any last words I want you to pass on to my old army comrades? I don't give a bloody damn about the 3rd Northumberland mob, Holmes, just untie me, you fool!

WATSON becomes VON BORK

Ha! How I pity these unsuspecting British idiots, sleeping so soundly in their beds! Soon the plague bacillus will have decimated their pitiful population, and as for those weaklings left alive, I will have a surprise in store for them all!

With the Mazarin Stone now in my possession, it will soon be time to harness its power and to summon down from above the horrors of the heights! How typical of the Englanders to be so blind as to ignore the mystery surrounding the mysterious deaths of Myrtle and the other aviators. Lulled into complacency, they refused to question the absence of Myrtle's head! I credit this pathetic nation's idiot eccentrics and their wild theories with more sense than the Government! Even when the lifeless body of Isadora Persano was found on the beach, wrapped within one of the air-kraken's tentacles, those imbeciles mistook it for the work of a *sea-worm*! But soon enough they will come to realise the catastrophe that will come crashing down upon their heads.

Yes, the horrors of the heights! Gigantic and monstrous, the kraken and the serpents of the air, the terrifying might of which will be drawn down by the power of the Mazarin Stone! These fearsome creatures will lay waste to the remnants of Britain, already devastated by the plague. With The Kaiser's enemies brought to their knees, there will be absolutely nothing to thwart Germany's master-plan.

It was so good of Herr Holmes to recover the Mazarin Stone for me. By now, The Creeper will be attending to the lighthouse keeper down below and straightening out his back for him.

And then The Creeper will take control of the lighthouse for himself and place the Mazarin Stone inside the light mechanism. The brilliancy of the Stone will be beamed direct into the darkling skies high above, and the death-ray will draw forth the aerial monsters from the heavens above – or rather, the Hell above!

I congratulate you, Herr Capitan in successfully duping the detective! Your masterful impersonation of Doctor Watson must have caused Herr Holmes great distress during his final moments. I regret not being able to watch him wrestle with the problem, of whether he ought to save his friend or those wretched Londoners instead!

And so, Herr Holmes chose friendship over loyalty to his nation! Tell me, Herr Capitan, did the detective realise the enormity of his foolishness in saving you? His weakness served to sign his city's death warrant! Did you reveal your true identity *before* or *after* the plague bacillus was released into the Thames? And did he beg for mercy before you despatched the *dump Kopf?*

VON BORK becomes WATSON

In between his pitiful sobs, he begged that I should impart these final words to you! Herr Holmes wishes you to know, Von Bork, that he believes there are one or two minor details you ought to have known before embarking upon your deception. The good doctor was formerly attached to the *Fifth* Northumberland Fusiliers, not the Third. It was there he sustained an injury to his *shoulder,* and not his knee. Furthermore, the *second* Mrs Watson is named Alice, *not* Mary. Oh, and incidentally, Watson's eyes are *blue*, and not brown.

WATSON reveals himself to be HOLMES

Allow me to introduce myself – I am Mr Sherlock Holmes. You ought to have realised Watson would sooner have suffered a thousand deaths before betraying his fellow countrymen. Shortly before Inspector Mac took your man into custody, I told him of these small and yet so crucial errors that had led to his incarceration.

I fear I must be the harbinger of more bad news, Von Bork. I released the *bogus* Watson, it is true, and of course the trebuchet was triggered – because I wanted it so! Having assessed the situation, I arranged the launch of Mordecai Smith to be steered into place, at a wharf close to the warehouse wherein *Watson* was imprisoned. I took careful aim, and fired at the launch's boiler, thereby causing an explosion.

Oh, I don't share your disregard for human life, Von Bork – Smith was warned well in advance and was out of harm's way.

With the boat merrily ablaze, I performed a simple calculation: I took the angle of trajectory, multiplied it by the square root of an isosceles triangle and divided that by

Guttenberg's principle of opposing forces in motion. Adjusting for the difference in equilibrium, I slashed at the rope and thereby released the triggering mechanism.

The plague-filled projectile was flung through the opened sky-light, sailed through the air and landed where I knew it would, to wit, into the fiery embrace of the burning launch. Consigned to the flames, the threat of the plague bacillus was nullified.

London lives to fight another day, Von Bork. There are one or two things you need to learn about the British spirit. Of course, if anything had happened to the *real* Watson, Von Bork, you would not be leaving this Zeppelin alive. As it is, I offer you a sporting chance, and trust you have honour enough to settle this like a gentleman… by the sword, Von Bork.

HOLMES *flourishes his walking-cane and uses it as a rapier - he duels with the unseen VON BORK*

I appear to have upset your plans, but you have come to Britain once too often, sir. However, once this is over, you'll be in no fit state to come again!

You have some small proficiency in swordsmanship, I see... So do I, however, and I mean to foil your schemes once and for all!

With a final flourish, HOLMES runs VON BORK through

HOLMES becomes VON BORK

You have first blood, Herr Holmes, but Germany will have the last laugh! You are already too late, for by now The Creeper will have gained control of the lighthouse and activated the Mazarin Stone! Your nation is mere moments away from being invaded by the horrors of the heights, and there is nothing you can do to stop them!

Forgive me if I leave you now, but I promised the English Channel I would drop in. Auf wiedersehen, Herr Holmes!

VON BORK leaps from the Zeppelin

SFX of a man's screams fading into the distance, and then a faint splash

Reverts to HOLMES

I would drop in... Those who claim the German has no sense of humour, were right.

Exit HOLMES

Voiceover, DR WATSON

Mere moments separated an unsuspecting England's night-time slumbers and an aerial invasion of those devilish creatures descending upon our green and pleasant land. Von Bork's insane device had harnessed the collective power of the Blue Carbuncle and the Mazarin Stone, and its supernatural force was now being beamed straight into the skies above. The heavens were bathed in a weird green light that cast a sickly pallor upon the English Channel below. Like the wildest imaginings of a feverish madman, those grotesque monstrosities broke through the clouds. Their sinuous tentacles slithered through the midnight air like so many giant serpents, reaching down to ensnare the land in their poisonous embrace. The vast, bulbous bodies of the creatures heaved and shuddered as they glided along the luminous beam of light that drew them ever onwards.

As the Zeppelin sped towards the creatures, Holmes noted the way in which the air-borne behemoths were positioning themselves in a line along the ray of greenish light being shone from the lighthouse. Seizing the steering-wheel of the aircraft, Holmes steered the S.S. Cormorant straight towards this calamitous death-ray and intercepted the monsters and the beam. He had noted peculiar physiological similarities between these horrors of the heights and the Portuguese Man o'War, whose symbiotic co-existences meant that where one led, the rest must follow.

With those terrifying creatures trailing behind the airship like some octopoid streamer and The Creeper operating Von Bork's death-ray in front, Sherlock Holmes drove the Zeppelin directly towards the lighthouse. Scant seconds before impact, Holmes left the steering-wheel and dived head-first into the ebony waters of the English Channel far below. Then with an earth-rending explosion, the Zeppelin collided with the lighthouse, sending an immense chain of fire that engulfed the creatures one after another. The night sky lit up as this aerial inferno returned the monsters to the hell from whence they'd sprung. All that remained of the lighthouse was a blazing pillar of smoke and flame, a funeral pyre for the brutish Hoxton Creeper. The tattered remains of the S.S. Cormorant were soon scattered by sea and air, like so many fragments of a bad dream, and the heavens presently lost that ghastly green hue.

But what had happened to Sherlock Holmes? Just as I had so nearly lost him all those years before at Reichenbach, at the hands of Moriarty, had my friend sacrificed his life for the greater good of the country he loved so deeply?

SFX. bees and the countryside

Enter SHERLOCK HOLMES

That really would have been my last bow, had I not been a strong swimmer. The same cannot be said for Von Bork, whose body was washed up onto the coast the following morning. I am happy to say that his nightmarish army has now joined him in the great hereafter, and with them, the thuggish Hoxton Creeper also.

Inspector Mac successfully found the genuine Watson, following the German prisoner's revelation of the good Doctor's whereabouts. He had been confined within an adjacent warehouse, one that had been formerly a manufactory of water-closets. Indeed, the solution to my Boswell's disappearance was alimentary enough.

So after that brief but not entirely uninteresting diversion, my bees once more have me all to themselves.

HOLMES *notices a telegram on the side-table*

A telegram – and it's from Mycroft!

Sherlock – STOP - Require urgent assistance – STOP – Navy in chaos – STOP - sightings of ghost ship *sending officers insane - STOP– Sailors claim to have seen* RMS Titanic *in Irish Sea – STOP – England needs you – STOP - Mycroft.*

Mrs Turner, I'm afraid I shall be away for a few days! Be sure to keep the home fires burning and the tea-pot warm till my return. It would seem that as long as my nation needs me, retirement must perforce wait. And perhaps Mrs

Watson would be able to spare the good Doctor for a week or so. It will be like old times with my Boswell at my side.

Indeed, with Watson once more, if only for a little while, there will be no need for me to be Sherlock Holmes - alone.

Exit **SHERLOCK HOLMES**

Sherlock Holmes and The Mazarin Malediction

Without Watson by my side, I am afraid I must rely upon my own humble abilities as a story-teller to relate the following curious episode in my career. You might recollect that some years ago, rather an embellished account was published in Strand Magazine. Readers at the time questioned its authenticity, and rightly remarked how different in tone it was to friend Watson's usual literary style. The reason being that the entire concoction had been the work of Watson's literary agent, Dr Conan Doyle.

Perhaps you will appreciate that such was Doyle's wholehearted immersion in the spiritualist movement, all other concerns of his had fallen by the wayside. He was experiencing undoubted financial pressures owing to the costs incurred by his travels and business ventures, designed to win new converts to his cause. I had retired and moved to my cottage upon the South Downs by that time, and Watson's health was in serious decline. Sadly, when publishers on either side of the Atlantic demanded more accounts of my old life in Baker Street with which to bolster sales of their books and magazines, friend Doyle found that the well had run dry. That is, at least as far as his client Watson was concerned.

Thus it came to pass, that Sir Arthur felt driven to write several tales for submission. He reasoned that he knew Watson's work sufficiently well enough to imitate. Previous attempts made by Doyle to establish his literary reputation with his own work met with indifference. Few bothered to read his historical works of fiction. He fared rather better with another client, Mr Edward Malone, whose work he edited. *The Lost World* and those other handful of tales concerning George Edward Challenger were quite popular. But Doyle was shrewd enough to realise that if he required considerable financial reward, then the public would settle for naught less than another selection of hitherto-unpublished tales from my criminal case-book.

One such tale concerned the theft of the Mazarin Stone. Doyle had sent me a telegram enquiring whether I would mind him adapting the case for a theatrical production in the city of Bristol, of all places. I told him that he may adapt it or adopt it or do whatever in God's name he wanted to do with it. I shared Mr Houdini's view that Doyle was undertaking a fool's errand with his espousal of his spiritualist beliefs. Doyle was spending money as quickly as he was earning it. But then after all, it was owing to Doyle's championing of friend Watson's literary efforts, that I was afforded a degree of celebrity. This assisted me immeasurably in strengthening my reputation as the world's first and only unofficial consulting detective, did it not? And so I relented and allowed Doyle to tamper with the facts of the Negretto Sylvius business as he saw fit.

Now, apropos the facts, it was I recall upon one overcast September morning in the year '98. Watson had married for the third time. Really, his selfishness knew no bounds where the fairer sex was concerned. I was alone once more. I was seated at the breakfast-table drinking my coffee and perusing that day's agony columns in the morning newspapers. I heard a commotion issuing from the hallway downstairs, and the strident tones of Mrs Hudson demanding the immediate surcease of the intruder's headlong flight up the seventeen steps of the stairwell to my room.

The door was flung open. Standing in the doorway was a young man of medium height. His ruddy complexion showed that his circulation was poor. His wild, disordered hair and laboured breathing showed he had undergone some crisis in the past few hours.

Pray you be seated, sir. You must be exhausted. You haven't slept and to wander aimlessly around town since the early hours is hardly conducive to good health. You must think of your asthma. I trust however that your train journey was pleasant enough. But what has impelled you to forsake the countryside?

The second half of a return train ticket, his dishevelled and unshaven appearance, the mud upon his boots, the sodden state of his overcoat following the early morning showers. You know my methods.

I allowed him to recover his composure. This is what he told me.

HOLMES becomes WARRENDER

You must excuse my dramatic entrance, Mr Holmes. You are correct. I fled Moorcroft Hall late last night before catching the very first train to London. I have been tramping the streets since arriving at Victoria first thing. I had to reach you in time to explain what has happened, Mr

Holmes. Any minute now, it might be too late. Any minute now, I may be arrested for a crime I did not commit.

I am innocent! Never mind what Lord Cantlemere would have you believe! There was a dinner party held there last night. I watched them from the grounds and peered in at the windows. I knew my way about the place. After all, I had used to be a footman there. My dear sister, Minnie, had used to be one of the maids there. I wish to God she had never set foot in the place. Then she would never have met that devil.

I am not a thief, Mr Holmes! I know that I am suspected, but I beg you to believe me!

Reverts to HOLMES

At that moment, the man's strange and disjointed narrative was interrupted by a knock upon the door. It was Inspector Hopkins of Scotland Yard. He was accompanied by several police officers, who seized the distrait young man seated at my table.

HOLMES becomes HOPKINS

Arthur Warrender, I arrest you in the name of the law! Take him downstairs, men. I'll be with you directly.

Well, Mr Holmes. I suspected he would make his way to you at some point. Lucky for us, we found him sooner rather than later. I don't know how much of his sorry tale he told you. It was the Sussex constabulary that alerted us to the crime. They felt it necessary to bring us in, given the severity of the crime. The theft of the Mazarin Stone! Moorcroft Hall is in a state of uproar.

It was Lord Cantlemere himself who pointed us in the right direction. He'd had to have Mr Warrender escorted off the premises just a few hours earlier. Oh, the young man had been making a general nuisance of himself since he was dismissed from their employ some weeks ago. They found him on the grounds again late last night.

It's true, the Mazarin Stone has yet to be found, Mr Holmes. Mr Warrender was searched on the premises, but it wasn't on his person. The local constabulary had yet to arrive when the young man made his escape. Does that not speak volumes for his guilt, Mr Holmes?

Once we have him safely under lock and key, I shall return to Moorcroft Hall and continue with the search. Priceless jewels do not simply disappear into thin air! It's only a matter of time, you mark my words.

Reverts to HOLMES

I asked Hopkins whether he would mind my accompanying him. There had been something about Warrender that had persuaded me of his innocence. However, one cannot theorize without data. The facts could only be gathered not there in Baker Street, but at the scene of the crime itself.

Moorcroft Hall was an austere and unprepossessing residence. The grounds were busy with local police-officers scouring for the clues their very zeal had already no doubt effaced. I was ushered into the library. There after a few moments, I was joined by Lord Canterville himself.

HOLMES becomes LORD CANTERVILLE

I have heard of you, Mr Holmes. You are an amateur, are you not? I fail to understand why you are interfering in the affairs of the official police-force. They have already arrested the thief, I take it. It will be but a matter of time until they find where the criminal has concealed it.

Surely even you are familiar with the Mazarin Stone, Mr Holmes. In terms of mere monetary value, it would fetch £100,000 at auction. However, that is beside the point. The Mazarin Stone is priceless. It was originally given as a gift by King Charles II to the Duchess of Mazarin. So attached to the jewel was the Duchess, that upon her death bed she heaped a curse upon anyone reckless enough, or foolish enough ever to steal that which was hers.

Over the years, several attempts have been made to abscond with the Stone. Only once was the miscreant successful in his enterprise. They found him dead, hanging by the neck from the boughs of Wyther's Oak not far from here. The Mazarin Stone was lodged in his throat. According to local legend, the spirit of the dead man is to be seen wandering the grounds, searching for the jewel that cost him his life.

I do not hold with such nonsense, Mr Holmes. It was not a ghost but a common flesh and blood criminal who is responsible for the crime. Inspector Hopkins has already apprehended the man responsible. All that remains now is to restore the Stone to its rightful place, here at Moorcroft. That is why I believe you are wasting your time, Mr Holmes. Leave detection to the professionals at Scotland Yard. You may be at liberty to ride upon their coat-tails in London, sir, but not here.

Reverts to HOLMES

I asked Hopkins what he had learned regarding the dismissal of Arthur Warrender from Moorcroft Hall. According to the other servants, he had taken to the drink following the death of his sister, Minnie. Minnie Warrender also had been employed at Moorcroft, as a waiting-maid. Unfortunately for her, this led to her falling under the power of the young nobleman, Count Negretto Sylvius.

According to Hopkins, Count Sylvius was a noted gambler, sportsman, game-shot and man-about-town. Little was known of his past, save that his people hailed from Southern Italy. Even in the brief amount of time he had moved within English society, he had managed to become embroiled in several romantic intrigues. One of these happened to involve the late Miss Warrender.

This enigmatic gentleman had been a guest at Moorcroft for some weeks. Hopkins had ascertained that Sylvius divided his time between Lord Cantlemere's home and his own London residence. Indeed, before the hour was out, I had the opportunity to meet with the Count in person.

HOLMES becomes COUNT NEGRETTO SYLVIUS

Ah, the servants have been gossiping I take it, correct?

What was the girl's name? Minnie Warrender! She had developed an absurd infatuation with me. Am I to be responsible for the actions of every silly young woman. She took her own life, you say. Yes, I think I recollect something Lord Cantlemere said, how unreliable these working classes can be. And good servants are so terribly difficult to come by!

In my native country, Mr Holmes, the servants are grateful and keep themselves to their proper stations in life. Yet here at Moorcroft, life is not so very different to that in my beloved Salerno. There I have my family and our villas. And yet I have my London residence also, Mr Holmes! Why conceal the wealth one has earned. Those who look on with the jealous eyes must grovel in the dust and bow down before their superiors, no?

Reverts to HOLMES

I remarked to Count Sylvius what a coincidence it was he should hail from Salerno. I happened to know of some people there and had used to correspond with one of Salerno's most notable citizens, the philosopher, Giuseppe Gilletti. Sadly, he had passed away but the previous year. Yes, Count Sylvius remembered him well. Signor Gilletti was remembered with great affection.

With that, Count Sylvius took his leave. He was to return to his London residence that same day, he said, to attend to important business.

From Hopkins, I learned that the Mazarin Stone had until the night before been kept inside the family safe. It was understood that the theft had taken place after everyone had retired for the night. The combination lock of the safe had proven to be of little consequence to the culprit. No actual evidence had been found to implicate young Warrender, save that he had been seen on the premises on the night of the burglary. When questioned as to why he was there, Warrender had responded that he blamed Count Sylvius for the death of his late sister. Upon discovering that the nobleman was staying at Moorcroft Hall, Warrender had trespassed with a view to denouncing him. However, Warrender had evidently already been in his cups and was inebriated. Even the most rudimentary safe would require a seasoned cracksman to have his senses about him. It seemed unlikely that Warrender would have possessed either the wherewithal or skills necessary to effect the theft.

Where, then, was the Mazarin Stone? Inspector Hopkins

and the local constabulary would manage without my presence for a while. I intended to return to London ahead of Count Sylvius. I wanted to discover what business exactly was taking him away from Moorcroft so suddenly.

Old Baron Dowson remarked the night before he was hanged, that in my case what the law had gained the stage had lost. Friend Watson would tell you that I never can resist a touch of the dramatic. And so it was not as myself, but rather in the guise of an old sporting man that I followed Count Sylvius later that day. I loitered on a street corner as I watched him leave 136, Moorside Gardens, then followed him at a distance.

From the respectable and well-heeled environs of Northwest London, Count Sylvius hailed a cab. I did the same, taking not the first, nor the second, but the third hansom that rattled along. Journeying toward the East End, Count Sylvius alighted close to the Whitechapel Road. I did the same, then continued to follow him. I was familiar with the area and soon realised whose company the nobleman sought.

A walk of a few minutes brought me to the disreputable premises of Ikey Sanders. Then my suspicions had been confirmed. Count Sylvius leave several minutes later. The expression upon his swarthy features suggested that his business meeting had not gone according to plan. Count Sylvius walked briskly along the street and hailed another cab. I decided I would also venture into the dingy property rented by Ikey Sanders, a stone-cutter of my acquaintance.

Several years before I had done Sanders a good turn by successfully proving his innocence when charged with assault. Therefore, I was soon able to elicit the information I needed.

HOLMES becomes IKEY SANDERS

Why, is that you, my dear Mr Holmes? I would not have recognised you at all if not for you telling me. You ought to have gone on the stage, you would have made a rare actor and no mistake. Yes, that was the Count Sylvius. His business here, sir? I trust you, Mr Holmes, and I know this will not go no further as I have a business to run and my overheads to think of, overheads to think of, Mr Holmes!

It was a stone he wanted me to cut up for him, but not just any stone, no, it was the *Stone, the Mazarin Stone! Word travels fast in my line of business. I may have, it is true, rather a philosophical approach to the law of the land, but to be embroiled in this affair would be too warm for me, Mr Holmes, too warm for me. I have a business to run, and overheads to think of, Mr Holmes. I might not make as much money on the outside as I would like. But I would make even less behind bars, eh?*

Reverts to HOLMES

That evening back at Baker Street, I telephoned Inspector Hopkins. He had returned to Scotland Yard leaving his Sussex counterparts to continue their investigations. The Stone had not been discovered, he told me. I responded that there was a very good reason why. I told him what I had seen apropos Count Sylvius.

My suspicions had been confirmed where this noble were concerned. The Count claimed to know well my Italian philosopher friend, the late Giuseppe Gilletti. But no such a person ever existed. There was no Giuseppe Gilletti. The case against poor Warrender was weak enough, and now it would fall apart completely. Yet I required actual incriminating evidence against the man who claimed to be a nobleman of Italian heritage.

There was something oddly familiar about the Count. His long, curved nose made him resemble a bird of prey. And his thin-lipped mouth, beneath the large, formidable moustache, betokened violence and cruelty in the extreme.

I had posted two of my Irregulars outside his home. A third kept me informed of the Count's actions. When I was notified that Sylvius had taken a cab to the Minories, there to visit old Straubenzee's workshop of all places, I took immediate action.

So it was, that before the hour was out, you may have observed an elderly, shabbily-attired woman also in the Minories, seated upon a bench and taking in the view. Once in a while, she would rummage inside her bag and withdraw a pear drop, on which she would suck meditatively. Then from Straubenzee's workshop, emerged Count Sylvius. Tucked underneath his arm was an oblong mahogany box, perhaps no larger than a violin case.

As the man walked through the Minories with a confident air, the woman dropped her parasol upon the ground. She endeavoured to stoop down to retrieve it, whereupon Sylvius picked it up and handed it back to her suavely. He tipped his top hat toward her and then swaggered away. The old woman looked after him thoughtfully.

Would it surprise you to know that the same baggy parasol currently stands propped against the wall in the adjoining room? It would have surprised Count Sylvius even more to know that the old woman to whom he had behaved so gallantly was none other than myself.

It was the connection between Count Sylvius and old Straubenzee that finally removed any doubt from my mind. I returned to Baker Street and divested myself of the costume. Then I telephoned Hopkins at the Yard.

Perhaps you are aware that Scotland Yard has its own museum. It contains the many and varied artefacts and curious disjecta membra of old cases they have collected over the years. Though I have always shunned publicity and would much rather Scotland Yard's Lestrade or Gregson took the credit for my successes, nonetheless, occasionally the case has been so well-known, such a cause celebre, this has proven to be impossible. Occasionally, the macabre souvenir and I have become synonymous. It was such an exhibit that I asked to be delivered to Baker Street then, in the company of Hopkins and four of his men.

So it came to pass, that a short while later that day, the wax dummy sculpted by the artist Tavernier, that had featured so prominently in the affair of the *Empty House,* was restored to its erstwhile position in the window of my rooms. I peered at the gaping hole in the forehead of the bust. This had been the damage wrought by the late, unlamented Colonel Sebastian Moran, and the single soft revolver bullet he had fired from his air-gun from the window of the building opposite.

This air-gun also was displayed in the Scotland Yard Museum. It had been the only one of its kind, a fine example of old Straubenzee's craftsmanship. But now another such weapon existed, and it was in the possession of Count Negretto Sylvius.

Hopkins and the police-officers were stationed in the adjoining room. I telephoned Count Sylvius and asked that he visit Baker Street that very evening. I wished to discuss with him a matter of grave importance concerning his immediate future, and the degree of personal liberty he was to enjoy therein. The nobleman understood my meaning perfectly well.

My rooms in Baker Street were in semi-darkness when

Sylvius walked in. Only the feeble glimmer from an oil-lamp allowed any sort of light. He closed the door quietly behind him and surveyed the room. He gave an audible gasp when he discerned Mr Sherlock Holmes seated facing the window. The detective was gazing outside, seemingly lost in thought.

Sylvius paused, then raised his heavy walking-cane and stole stealthily toward his nemesis. With a ferocious downwards swing, Sylvius struck at the figure again and again. However, when he examined more closely his bloody handiwork, and peered at the cleft skull of the lifeless body, the Count was disappointed and outraged in equal measure. He scooped up the pulped remains of the smashed waxen bust, cast them to the floor.

The strains of a Hoffman barcarolle were coming from somewhere inside the room. And then Sylvius heard the voice of a dead man. It was the voice of the late Colonel Sebastian Moran.

SFX of violin music and VOICE of MORAN

You fool! Any son of mine ought to know better than to fall for one of Holmes's tricks. I am disappointed in you, James.

I was ashamed of you in life. And now I am ashamed of you in death.

Sylvius turned and saw the spirit of Moran standing before him. From the corner of his eye, the Count noticed a revolver lying on the table. He snatched it and fired once, twice, three times at the eerie figure.

James, you are an idiot to suppose bullets can harm one who is already dead. I am amazed you were able to steal the Mazarin Stone and remain undetected. Little wonder Ikey Sanders turned you away.

Count Negretto Sylvius, or rather, James Moran, staggered back, dropping the gun as he did so.

He stammered his response.

HOLMES as JAMES MORAN/SYLVIUS

I have the Stone, but Van Seddar will cut it up for me this very night. He says it can be Amsterdam before Sunday. Good God, father, how can it be you? You are dead!

Reverts to HOLMES

Suddenly, Moran sprung toward the other figure, his walking-cane raised. He went to strike down the form before him. But Moran neatly parried the thrust, then dealt a stunning straight right to the opponent's jaw. Moran fell to the floor. Moran spoke.

You can come out now, Hopkins!

The men from Scotland Yard emerged from the adjoining room. The dazed Moran was dragged to his feet and handcuffed. Hopkins searched the prisoner. He withdrew his hand and held aloft his prize.

The great yellow Mazarin Stone, seventy-seven carats, and without flaw! I took the Stone and held it toward the gaslight. Mr Moran, I take great exception to your cavalier disregard for my poor old bust. It had used to be such a pretty little thing. Tavernier, the French modeller, made it. He is as good at waxwork as Straubenzee is at airguns. However, I thank you for giving me this opportunity of freeing the country from a pest, which devastates it and lives on the population.

Do you know what I keep inside this book? You. You're all here, every action of your vile and disreputable life. The real facts as to the death of Miss Minnie Warrender. The story of young Arbothnot, who was found drowned in the

Regents Canal. The real facts as to the death of old Mrs. Harold, who left you her entire estate, which you so rapidly gambled away. It's all here, Mr Moran. In spite of what I said earlier, before you so gracefully fell to the floor, I think your father the Colonel would have been proud of your achievements. But every man meets his Waterloo eventually. Hopkins, take him away. Oh, but before you do, perhaps you will be so kind as to switch off the music in the other room. Ah, yes, these modern gramophones! Wonderful invention! Oh, I trust you will not mind my retaining possession for a while longer of the Stone. A lesson in humility needs to be learned, and this will facilitate matters wonderfully well.

I then changed out of my phosphorus-daubed costume and made myself presentable once more. I was expecting one more visitor that night.

When Lord Cantlemere arrived, he cut a gloomy figure. His whiskers gleamed with a shiny blackness, at variance with his rounded shoulders and feeble tread. I went to take his overcoat from his shoulders, but he shrugged me aside.

Lord Cantlemere, I am hopeful of recovering the Stone, it is true. But there remain certain obstacles that I may have difficulty overcoming. You see, Lord Cantlemere, we can no doubt frame a case against the actual thieves. But the question is, how shall we proceed against the receiver? Now, what would you regard as final evidence against the receiver? The actual possession of the stone. You would arrest him upon that? You would?

In that case, my dear sir, I shall be under the painful necessity of advising your arrest.

HOLMES becomes LORD CANTLEMERE

You take a great liberty, Mr. Holmes. In fifty years of official life I cannot recall such a case. I am a busy man, sir engaged upon important affairs, and I have no time or taste for foolish jokes. I may tell you frankly, sir, that I have never been a believer in your powers. I have always been of the opinion that the matter was far safer in the hands of the regular police force. Your conduct confirms all my conclusions. I have the honour, sir, to wish you good-evening!

Reverts to HOLMES

My Lord! One moment! To actually go off with the Mazarin stone would be a more serious offence than to be found in temporary possession of it. Kindly put your hand in the right-hand pocket of your overcoat.

The elderly aristocrat reached inside, and to his astonishment, found he was holding the missing jewel in the palm of his hand.

My old friend Watson will tell you that I have an impish habit of practical joking. Also that I can never resist a dramatic situation. I took the liberty of putting the stone into your pocket at the beginning of our interview. No doubt, Lord Cantlemere, your pleasure in telling of this successful result in the exalted circle to which you return will be some small atonement for my practical joke.

HOLMES as CANTLEMERE

We are greatly your debtors, Mr. Holmes. Your sense of humour may, as you admit, be somewhat perverted, and its exhibition remarkably untimely. But at least I withdraw any reflection I have made upon your amazing professional powers.

Reverts to HOLMES

Perhaps on your way out, Lord Cantlemere, you will good enough to ask my housekeeper Mrs Hudson to prepare something for me to eat. I have dined upon nothing other than a handful of pear drops during the past forty-eight hours. I must break my fast, lest the Mazarin Malediction you spoke of claims another victim.

The Giant Rat of Sumatra

I recall that it was a chilly November's evening when Watson and I were seated before a fire at 221b Baker Street. I was in a retrospective mood. There had been few cases in the last six months to test my powers. I considered myself a brain, and the rest a mere appendix. But without work, what is there to live for? The criminal element had lost all its sense of panache and initiative. At best, they could only commit such crimes as even Scotland Yard could solve. Lamentable!

I could sense that Watson was becoming nervous at my restlessness. No doubt he would have endeavoured to conceal my morphia and cocaine from me if he had been able to find them. But I had foreseen his well-intentioned actions and had hidden the small Morocco case and its contents from his prying eyes.

At that moment there came the pounding footsteps of a heavily-set man running up the stairs. A mariner, obviously, judging from the rhythm of his feet. Years had been spent upon the rolling seas. Evidently of the merchant service, given such lack of calm and discipline. The Royal Navy would never countenance that.

The door opened and the sailor stood before us. He was in uniform, the blue faded from long wear, but clean and pressed.

Pray tell us of your difficulties, sir. Nothing less than murder, surely, would cause a man of your rank to come in person, and in such haste.

HOLMES becomes BOWMAN

Two murders, Mr. Holmes. And cannibalism into the bargain. My name is Peter Bowman, and I am the first mate of the Matilda Briggs of Brixham. We sailed a month ago from the island of Sumatra with a cargo of mahogany and copra. The captain, Mr. Blake, is also the owner of the vessel and we ply to and from the China Seas, carrying whatever cargo is profitable.

The first evening we docked at the port of Panang on Sumatra. A Chinaman, Mr. Lee, came aboard. He and Captain Blake spent a couple of hours talking together in his cabin. The next night the captain gave us all shore leave and said he'd stand the watch himself. This was unusual of him. Captain Blake was a strict man, and one for discipline. When we got back early in the morning, I was told that Mr. Lee was shipping some cargo with us and would be sailing with us to London.

This cargo was already aboard when I got back from shore leave. It was about twenty barrels of something heavy. Captain Blake said the barrels contained some kind of ore. I didn't ask any more. And Mr. Lee hardly said a word to anyone.

It wasn't a happy voyage back, sir. None of us liked to go into the cargo hold. It seemed very close down there, and we didn't like it. Well, we were about three weeks into the voyage when the captain died. It was a rough night. I was on watch and the captain was in the wheelhouse. He didn't rightly trust anybody else with his ship, I suppose. Anyway, I took a lantern and checked below. Suddenly, we went broadside to the waves. I was almost thrown overboard. The bo'sun, Peters, got to the wheel and brought us back on course.

I got to the wheelhouse as soon as I could. Inside I found the captain dead on the floor, in a pool of blood. He seemed to have been stabbed right through the nape of his neck. It must have cut his spine and killed him at once. I rolled him over to look at the face. Mr Holmes, I've been at sea all my life and seen many grim sights, but nothing to match this. His left cheek seemed to have been cut and chewn away! There was nothing but the red jaw and the white teeth grinning up at me.

The body was buried at sea the next morning. So far from port and at those latitudes we had no choice.

I took charge of the ship. I questioned every member of crew but got nowhere. No one had heard anything untoward. But as I said, the captain was a hard man and several of the crew had cause to dislike him. The master-at-arms, Bailey, had had arguments with him. But I cannot believe he would mutilate a man like the captain was. A couple of the Lascars too, I questioned pretty hard. And then of course there was Mr. Lee.

According to him, he was in his cabin asleep. He had heard nothing and seen nothing. Still, it was a good ten minutes after the ship yawed that he appeared on deck. He didn't look half-asleep either.

I didn't have enough cause to put anyone in irons. All I could do was write it all down in the log, and issue orders that all deck duties after dark were to be done in pairs. The *next day I read the service over the captain and sent him over the side wrapped in sailcloth. We had another ten day's sailing to London. We docked early this morning. I sent a telegram to Captain Blake's brother telling him of the accident. He needs to come and sort out the new ownership. I'm not much with words, sir. Then early tonight, we had our second killing.*

It was about seven o'clock. I was in the captain's cabin when I heard a scream. I dashed out into the companionway. Another scream, from 'tweendecks. By the time I got there, I was already too late. It was Bailey, the master-at-arms. He was still in his hammock, but it was wrapped around him, trussing him up. And from his body great drips of blood fell and splashed onto the lower deck. The body was untangled. There were four parallel slashes of a knife across his chest, not very deep. They weren't enough to kill him. What did kill him was a great tear in his stomach. A very nasty death, Mr. Holmes.

Anyway, there is little more to tell. We called the police. The men from Scotland Yard are on the ship now. I came here right away, Mr Holmes. I don't believe the police can find who killed my shipmates, but maybe you can.

BOWMAN reverts to HOLMES

A four-wheeler was summoned. Bowman, Watson and I made haste to the docks. It was a long journey, mostly passed in silence. Once arrived, the moorings of the *Matilda Briggs* already were crowded by inquisitive onlookers. A constable kept them well back from the gangplank.

Lestrade was in charge of the investigation. We walked up the gangplank and a policeman led us to the captain's cabin. Within were the Inspector, a burly constable and Mr Lee.

HOLMES becomes LESTRADE

Ah, Mr Holmes! Delighted to see you here. And you, Doctor Watson, of course. I'm afraid that you won't find anything of interest. All rather straightforward. No, we shan't be requiring assistance this time, Mr Holmes. Mr Lee here has been placed under arrest. A thorough search was made of everyone's baggage on board. The sailors had only their sea-chests. But Mr. Lee here had a very interesting collection. That bottle appears to contain a powerful sleeping draught. Those leather straps and buckles would hold a mad bull. A running noose could obviously be employed to strangle someone. And that fishing trident has traces of blood upon the tips. The curved knife we found up his sleeve must be the murder weapon.

LESTRADE reverts to HOLMES

Lestrade had been his usual zealous self. However, he was singly unable to explain why Mr. Lee had brought such a murderous collection abroad at all. And furthermore, why so many of them? I asked Mr Lee to explain himself. He said nothing.

With Lestrade's permission, Watson and I inspected the cargo hold. There was always the possibility of a stowaway. The cargo hold is the only place on a small ship where he could possibly conceal himself. The Inspector was incredulous. What man could stay hidden for a month and not leave traces? And what would he eat? Nonetheless, I wanted to examine the space all the same.

Below decks it was stuffy and smelt of timber and the sickly scent of copra. With a lantern in one hand and my lens in the other, I scoured the hold.

Lestrade! Look at this!

I was standing at the stern of the vessel, where the ends of the giant timbers were visible. They had been roughly squared off with an adze. Many of them were fully five feet across at the widest point. There were many gaps in the wood-pile. I directed their attention to the largest one of these, perhaps two feet square. The smell of vermin was evident.

Lestrade peered into the hole.

As LESTRADE

Rats, Mr Holmes! There's been a regular nest of them! There's straw and droppings all over the place. What's that, you say there was only one rat! Why should anyone want to keep a rat down here? What good is a rat to anyone, anyway?

Observe the size of the droppings, Inspector, and the length of its claw marks on the wood. I would estimate that the rat is no less than four feet long! That is why it had to be kept in secret. The markings leave no doubt. This wooden lattice had sealed the creature within its quarters. It was being cared for by Mr. Lee. I have found strands of red silk caught on the edges of the timber. The silk would appear to match the robe he wears. There is also a trail of copra leading to this den.

I turned to face Mr Lee. At night you went below. You fed the rat from one of the bales of copra. Rats possess a great tenacity for life, so a few weeks in the dark would not do the beast any great harm. You wished to bring it alive to England. For what purpose, may I ask? Come, Mr Lee. Do you not realise what this means? It is clear that it was the rat that carried out the killings. Consequently, your life at least is not forfeit. It is entirely in your own interests to give us more details.

At last Mr Lee spoke.

HOLMES as LEE

I bring rat. I take him to British Museum and sell him. Your scientists very interested in this rat. Captain Blake know all about him and agree. Poor Captain Blake. There was great storm. I stumble when I give rat food. It rush past me on to deck. When I get to Captain, it too late. I put rope on rat while it feed. Prick it with trident until it leave him.

Tonight I try to move rat. I try to give rat sleeping stuff, but it very angry, very powerful. It spring at me and knock me down. I think it kill me, but I hit it with cage door. Then it run away and kill first man it find. Bailey. Now rat gone. I know not where.

LEE reverts to HOLMES

A vicious killer was on the loose in the East End. Lestrade looked appalled. He returned to Scotland Yard to consult with his superiors. Mr Lee was to remain aboard the *Matilda Briggs*. Watson and I meanwhile, went back to Baker Street.

Over the next few days, Watson was fretful and restless. He was never happy sitting for long periods without action. As for myself, I was busy cross-referencing a large ordnance map of the East End with divers engineering drawings and technical blueprints. The map I had pinned to the wall and had commenced to draw thereon a network of lines in various colours.

Watson knew me well enough not to interrupt me. At last I explained to him my reasoning. Where does any rat hide? In the drains and sewers under the streets, of course. It matters not that our rat is so much larger, its instincts will remain the same. The different colours represent different sizes and depths of pipes. The symbols represent the different sorts of access to those pipes.

From time to time we would receive a note from Lestrade, detailing the sightings of the great rat. Within a day of its escape it had become the terror of the East End. Reports reached us of dogs and cats found eviscerated and half eaten. However, it was likely that the creature preferred to scavenge rather than to kill.

In many ways, however, the rat would be easier to ensnare than a human quarry. True, he possessed great speed and could access tunnels where we cannot or dare not follow. But the creature could not reason. Once we were aware of its habits, then it could be captured.

It was in fact the next day that I received the last piece of the puzzle. I had successfully located the creature's lair. It was a single conduit, marked with a blue line on the map. It was an overflow drain, taking excess flood water direct from Limehouse to the Thames. The coming of dusk found Watson and me in Dangerfield Street in Limehouse. A foetid reek emanated from the drains. It was here that I surmised the rat would make its nocturnal foray.

I put my hand inside the canvas bag I carried and drew forth a quantity of grain. I scattered this in the way that fishermen lay ground-bait, enough to awaken the creature's appetite, but not enough to satisfy it. This done, Watson and I took up sentry duty in the upstairs room of a house that stood further down the lane. From the window we could both observe a shed. Inside I had placed a quantity of half-rotted lamb. I had changed the hinges to the shed's door. A length of black cotton from the meat held this open. If the thread should snap, the door would instantly shut and latch.

It was close to eleven o'clock when something at last happened. The door slammed shut, and we could hear the sound of something large thudding against the shed walls from within. We leaped down the stairs, out the door and across the alley. One of the planks was already splintering outwards. With one end of a fishing net in my hand, I flung the other to friend Watson. I threw open the shed door.

There came a furious scrabbling as the rat wheeled about and dashed outside. The net was wrapped securely around the animal. I looked with delight at the rat, which still struggling furiously. I freely own that Watson seemed horrified by what he saw. The rat was fully four feet long, and dark grey in colour. Its large yellow incisor teeth were bared, and its long claws jutted and jabbed through the netting.

I went into the shed and returned at once dragging a large and stout cage. I had had this made up by a local carpenter that very day. With some degree of effort, Watson and I eventually confined the animal within. With Watson on guard, I secured a cart on which to convey the creature back to the Royal Docks. After all, the rat did rightfully belong to Mr Lee. It was our duty to return the creature to its owner.

In less than an hour, we found ourselves again at the moorings of the *Matilda Briggs*. Mr Lee was standing on deck.

A very good morning to you, Mr. Lee! I have great pleasure in informing you that we have found your rat, and it reposes safe and well within this cage.

At this, Lee descended the gangplank and walked over to the cage. He lifted a corner of the sacking and looked for a long moment at the beast. He bowed deeply, thanked us, and we took our leave of him.

On the way back to Baker Street, Watson ventured to suggest that a circus would have paid Mr Lee far more than the British Museum to acquire the rat. I scoffed at the suggestion.

You surely did not believe that flimsy story, Watson? The British Museum would no doubt be interested, but they prefer their animals dead and stuffed. The Zoo would have been a better suggestion. Mr Lee went to great trouble and danger to bring the rat to our shores alive. He must have anticipated a large profit. Captain Blake also must have expected to be well paid. There is a person behind all this, Watson. A person who wanted the giant rat to be brought to him alive and in secret.

I believed Lee would want to collect his money and leave the country as soon as possible.

So it was that the next night saw us again at the Royal Docks, observing the *Matilda Briggs*. It was at eight o'clock that the cage containing the giant rat was being unloaded from the vessel. Then the first of a succession of large barrels began to be rolled down the gangplank.

I reminded Watson that these barrels contained pitchblende, also known as uraninite. When we were aboard the ship, I had managed to pry a sample from one of the barrels. As far as I was aware, the stuff possessed no unique properties. The cart was soon loaded. Mr. Lee took his place beside the driver, and they set off. Watson and I followed on foot. The speed of a cart is so slow as to make pursuit in a cab conspicuous.

After three hours, the cart halted in front of an imposing town house in Harley Street. Watson told me these were Dr. Trelawney's premises. Trelawney specialised in the science of nutrition. He was greatly in demand by the quality to advise them on their diet when they felt out of sorts, Watson added.

Mr Lee pulled at the bell, and Trelawney himself answered. The cargo was unloaded and carried into the house. At last the job was done. The carter returned to his seat. Lee bowed low to the doctor, then turned and climbed up beside the driver. Trelawney raised his hand in farewell and went back inside.

I walked straight to the front door also and rang the bell. After a short time Trelawney appeared, looking suspicious.

HOLMES becomes TRELAWNEY

Good evening, gentlemen. You are aware no doubt that it is almost midnight? I trust your business is urgent. Your name, sir? I have heard of you, Mr. Holmes. I am grateful on this occasion for your intervention. I have been following the situation in the papers, and I feared that the rat would be killed, or even disappear for good. Please step inside.

Now, gentlemen, you must understand that I tell you everything in complete confidence. Please come with me.

Reverts to HOLMES

Trelawney led the way to the third floor. There he unlocked a heavy door, behind which was a large room set up as a laboratory. Cages for experimental animals occupied one of the short walls, there were shelves of chemicals and reagents, and so forth. The cage containing the giant rat was on the floor. The rat stared at us and bared its teeth.

The only unusual feature was a table in the centre of the room bearing a large plaster relief model of the island of Sumatra. It seemed to be studded with many slim wooden rods. Trelawney continued.

HOLMES as TRELAWNEY

May I ask you first to look at these specimens. Hypertropia, Mr Holmes. A gigantic snail, embalmed. An oak leaf almost a foot long. The skull of a gigantic man. The desiccated corpse of a dung beetle as large as a cat. These were collected in a certain area of the island of

Sumatra by my agent, Mr. Lee. He is a leading apothecary in Penang, and I entered correspondence with him many years ago. One day, he sent me a specimen of that plant fully ten times the size of any other I had seen. He explained that he had discovered an area within the interior of the island where much of the flora and fauna had grown to gigantic size. I offered to pay him well for further examples.

You will observe that the whole natural kingdom is represented. From this it can be inferred that giantism must be stimulated by some feature of the environment. I spared no effort in finding what that might be. Now I believe I have discovered the active substance.

As HOLMES

I interrupted him. Pitchblende. Of course! Trelawney looked somewhat crestfallen.

Reverts to TRELAWNEY

Oh, you already know, Mr Holmes. Small quantities of it will be leached into the surrounding soil by the rains, and so taken up by plants. These will be eaten by herbivorous animals, which will in turn be eaten by carnivores. A good supply of pitchblende is stored in my cellars. I mean to conduct a series of experiments. The rat shall prove invaluable in my research. Once compete, we will be able to breed giants at will.

Can you not see what a difference this will make to the lives of the common man? I will have helped banish hunger from the world forever! The race will be in the verge of a golden age.

Reverts to HOLMES

Sadly, the greatest schemes of Dr Trelawney were not to be. A year later, I received a letter from this visionary. He warned of the dreadful dangers his experiments had revealed to him. He had discovered that the presence of pitchblende often resulted in grotesque deformities in the offspring. Some were giants, but others were simply monstrous. Most of these creatures did not live long.

Furthermore, Trelawney had developed cancer as a result of his work with the pitchblende. He had but weeks to live. He'd destroyed his notes and specimens, including the giant rat. This he had poisoned and disposed of in a hospital incinerator.

The Adventure of the Amazonian Explorer

The tale that was brought to my attention that morning in Baker Street was certainly unique. My visitor, Sir Joseph Dalton Hooker, came to me knowing he dare not risk putting the facts before the official police force.

HOLMES becomes SIR JOSEPH

It is the recent death of John Anderson that concerns me greatly, Mr Holmes. Few naturalists had explored South America as extensively. He did a good deal of work for Kew Gardens. There are certain matters relating to his decease that I would like you to investigate with the utmost discretion.

He died two days ago. He was found dead in his conservatory. The immediate cause of death was loss of blood. A number of the giant Amazonian leeches which he bred in the conservatory had attached themselves to him. They had drained him of so much blood, he died. He had bred these creatures for research purposes. He wished to recreate the conditions of the Amazon forest floor as closely as possible. He imported the most common Amazonian insects, then the lizards and so on, that feed off the insects, and various plants and fungi. Over three hundred separate species of plant and animal life. A living laboratory if you will.

Of course, leeches generally do not pose a threat to a grown man. There are documented cases of men getting drunk in leech habitats and being found dead the next morning, of course. But usually, the leeches will be noticed and easily removed.

Not that John Anderson was drunk or drugged. At least, that is what we believe. But this is only what I have been told by his wife and servants. But I have known him for many years and know that he drank only a little wine and took no drugs. Furthermore, he was quite alone in the conservatory. The door was locked on the inside. His assistant had to smash a pane of glass to gain entry.

Mr Holmes, the police believe that he must have suffered an attack of dizziness and fallen. John suffered from malaria as a consequence of his travels. They suggest that he fainted from this and died when the leeches drained his blood. An accidental death. However, there are certain circumstances that make me wish to have the death investigated more thoroughly.

You will be aware, no doubt, that up to about twenty years ago, the country of Brazil had a monopoly on rubber production. This was a major part of their economy after all. Those who endeavoured to circumvent this monopoly were dealt with severely. But in 1876, a young adventurer named Henry Wickham brought some thousands of seeds of the species Hevea to us at Kew. We succeeded in germinating many of them.

The truth however is that the seeds were obtained by John Anderson and smuggled home by him in amongst other specimens. He was able to confound the Brazilian customs officials. He could not however have his own role in the matter made public as he would never again be able to return to the Amazon. Our consul found young Wickham, a fellow who had been sent to the upper Amazon by his family. In return for a sum of money, he agreed to take the credit for obtaining the seeds. He was boastful, and I do believe he even convinced himself that he was genuinely the man responsible. The joke was perhaps carried too far when he was later knighted for the exploit. I think it possible that the truth became known, and a Brazilian patriot decided to assassinate Anderson. Honour was at stake. It is not uncommon for a man to spend his whole life to even a score.

Naturally, I cannot tell the police any of this. The story of Wickham's exploits is so widespread. We would be branded liars. This entire matter must be treated with the utmost discretion and secrecy, Mr Holmes. Many reputations depend upon it.

Reverts to HOLMES

Sir Joseph was good enough to arrange an introduction to the widow of the deceased. He would tell Mrs Anderson that I was an expert in tropical diseases. And so it was the very next day that friend Watson and I journeyed to the Anderson home, near to Kew Gardens.

Mrs Anderson was a woman of striking appearance. Tall and dignified, she had been much younger than her late husband. She was dressed in mourning, of course. She invited us to be seated. I explained that we were there to investigate the death of her husband. His widow merely shrugged.

HOLMES becomes MRS ANDERSON

My husband had been suffering from some dizzy spells lately, although he refused to go to the doctor. He said it was merely his old trouble, malaria, and he would dose himself with quinine. It is clear to me that he fainted while he was alone and so was killed by those repulsive creatures of his.

Disease flourishes in the hot climate. My husband spent much time in the Amazon. I first met him in Manaos. My father was a government official. John came to him to get some papers, but he fell ill with the fever. I acted as his nurse. Through that we fell in love, although he was much older than me. We married and he brought me to London. Since then there have been other visits to Brazil and other illnesses.

When the funeral arrangements are made, I will return to my own people. I am tired of this cold wet city. I long for the festivals, and the dancing, and the generous friendship that you will find in my own land. I have not returned since my husband took me away and brought me to England. I do not like the sea crossing and I cannot share my husband's interest in the worms that writhe in the mud. Finally, they have killed him.

Reverts to HOLMES

I asked the widow if we could be shown her husband's study. She led us into an adjoining room. Books on all aspects of natural history ranged the shelves. On one corner of the desk was a large cabinet photograph of his wife as a young woman. On the other, a matching photograph of an upright man in naval uniform. I asked Mrs Anderson who that gentleman was.

HOLMES as MRS ANDERSON

That is the former King of Brazil, Dom Pedro. He befriended my husband in his younger days. The King was always most anxious to see the Amazon opened up to trade. Then of course he was deposed by the army. Not that I care. I am just a woman and have no interest in such things. My husband had political views, although not strong ones.

Reverts to HOLMES

Watson and I then examined the scene of the tragedy. Mrs Anderson did not accompany us. She could no longer stand the place. Indeed, she said she intended to have it torn down as soon as possible. She rang a bell for the maid and told her to take us to Mr. Doggett.

The maid led us to a small and crowded workroom at the rear of the house. As for Doggett, he described himself as Anderson's assistant and added that he had originally raised the alarm. He was an alert young man, with obvious energy. He took us to where the body had been found. He led us to the foot of the gardens, close to the river, where there stood a very large conservatory.

HOLMES becomes MR DOGGETT

This is our terrarium, gentlemen. It was designed by Mr. Anderson to mimic the conditions of the Amazon basin as closely as possible. He had close connections with Kew Gardens and spent a good deal of time there studying the construction and heating methods of its Palm House. This door is the only entrance.

Yes, the heat inside here is rather extreme. This stove is always kept burning. It has to be refilled twice a day, early morning and late afternoon. We damp it down overnight. It serves to heat the air and to take the chill off the water.

Now along this pathway, we come to the pool. You hear the insects no doubt, though you cannot see them. This is where I found Mr. Anderson. He was lying mainly under that bush, and with his feet in the pool. He was a terrible sight with the leeches stuck to him. They were quite engorged with his blood. Several of them had fastened on to the bare skin around his neck. I dragged him at once to the entrance and ran for help. I brought salt back with me from the kitchen and got rid of the leeches, but it was all too late. It was about seven o'clock in the evening. I had only come in to attend to the stove, you understand.

Mr Anderson's usual routine was to visit the terrarium after lunch and spend the afternoon there. So I suppose he could have been lying here for up to five hours. When I arrived the door was fastened but the key was in the lock, so I knew he must be inside. I shouted and knocked on the glass but there was no reply. I suppose I feared some accident might have happened, so I broke one of the panes and reached through for the key.

He preferred to work alone most of the time. He locked the door as well, to make sure he was undisturbed. Mr. Anderson worked closely with Kew but was entirely independent of them. He financed all his expeditions himself. This research was his hobby, his life's work. He told me often he considered himself a lucky man. Not that he was wealthy as such. There is no extravagance in the house, and very little entertaining.

Reverts to HOLMES

With Doggett's help we now explored the whole inside perimeter of the terrarium. I checked especially closely the points where the stream entered and exited. The surrounding soil showed no signs of disturbance. We went back to the entrance area, and I checked the floor carefully. Ah! I reached into a dark corner and brought out the corpse of a small frog. Its lifeless body was brightly patterned with yellow and black stripes. *Rana palmipes*, the Amazon River Frog. Doggett mentioned they were kept for the snakes and larger animals to feast upon. But why was the body so far from the foliage?

Doggett looked a little taken aback. He suggested perhaps the creature had been ill and had crawled away to die. Yes, no doubt. I returned the body to the undergrowth.

I asked if I might take a few of the leeches away with me for examination. Doggett felt there could be no objection to this. Indeed, he repeated what Mrs Anderson had already said, that she intended to demolish the terrarium. The specimens would be destroyed in any event. He left us for a short while and returned with a small coconut-fibre bag. He led the way back to the water and deftly stuffed the bag with pond weed. The leeches would stay alive for at least another day if kept inside this makeshift environment in miniature.

With Watson's assistance, I carefully picked a half-dozen or so of the leeches from the surrounding vegetation.

When we returned to the house, we found Mrs. Anderson in the company of a young man of swarthy appearance. He rose and bowed, smiling. He was, his hostess informed us, Señor Fernando Gomez, a friend of the family. We exchanged pleasantries affably enough. He told me he was a diplomat, and the commercial attaché for his embassy. His main concern was to encourage trade between our two nations. That day, however, he had come to convey his personal sorrow and condolences to Mrs. Anderson.

And with that we took our leave. We took the train back and returned to Baker Street. I spent the evening immersed in my reference books. My knowledge of Brazil required vast improvement if I was to unravel the intricacies of this affair. Watson had the good sense to leave me alone with my thoughts and my research.

I left early the next morning to visit St Bartholomew's Hospital. I sent word to Watson instructing him to meet me there at midday. The look of horror when he entered the laboratory in which I was conducting my experiment was to be expected perhaps. I had removed my shirt and placed several of the leeches upon my arms. Already the creatures were swollen with my blood. Beside me was a basin of water, with more of the leeches inside it.

I meant to explore their behaviour. The European medicinal leech is vastly different in size to its Amazonian cousin of course, which can grow to a full eighteen inches in length. But in all essential features, both are identical. I had been observing its method of attack. It first attaches its large tail-end sucker, then twists its body and applies the sucker on its head to the skin. Finally it makes an incision with its teeth and feeds. When it is satiated with blood, it falls from the host body. This takes about twenty minutes with the European leech and perhaps forty minutes with the Amazonian leech.

Inspecting the incisions and the creatures' mouthparts under a magnifying glass, I found that they have three jaws set with many small teeth. Therefore the wound it makes is shaped like the letter *Y*. Furthermore, in its saliva are substances to dull sensation, to dilate the victim's blood vessels to increase the flow, and to prevent the blood from clotting. Truly a remarkable creature!

I would send my results to Dr. Cronin. He was to conduct the post-mortem on John Anderson. It would enable him to determine which of the wounds on the deceased were caused by the leeches. One important thing I had learned was that leeches will not, or perhaps cannot, feed on the dead. It was therefore certain that Anderson was alive for some time, perhaps for as long as one hour. This in itself ruled out any theory of a heart attack or sudden death by another cause.

Watson kindly waited whilst I applied salve and plasters to my wounds. Once I was properly attired, we took a cab to Wardour Street. Arriving at a certain disreputable-looking restaurant, we went inside. The proprietor was expecting me, and he led us to the only occupied table. The two men already seated stood and bowed to us. These gentlemen were Pedro Funari and Antonio de Moura.

Gentlemen, you oblige me by taking me into your confidence. I hope that we will be able to exchange information to our mutual advantage. May I introduce my friend and confidante Dr. Watson. Watson, these gentlemen are of the Brazilian Royalist party in exile. Let us fortify ourselves with food before we speak of our business. I am looking forward to trying the delicacies of your native land.

After the meal, de Moura spoke.

HOLMES becomes De MOURA

We are loyal to his majesty Dom Pedro, the rightful ruler of Brazil. In 1889 he was forced to abdicate by the army. The church was against him because he acted against some corrupt bishops who lived at the expense of the poor. John Anderson supported the King's actions. He was his trusted friend.

After the king was overthrown, Anderson became part of our movement. His journeys to Brazil took him through the port of Belem at the mouth of the Amazon, and to Manaos where he had relatives by marriage. There he would meet with friends of the king. He took messages, money and essential supplies back and forth. We fear he was discovered and murdered by an assassin sent by the army. I know not how he was betrayed. I cannot believe it was one of our company. We are all faithful to the death.

Reverts to HOLMES

It soon became clear that they meant to reveal as little as possible. Most probably the Brazilian government would have had no hesitation in executing or imprisoning those working against their state. And so Watson and I took our leave.

Mrs Anderson must have known of all we had been told. Yet you will recall that she claimed that her husband had no strong political opinions. She would have no reason to protect his name. No Englishman would think the worse of him for helping those of another country gain their freedom. She wished to conceal the matter from us for some reason. I reasoned it concerned the *manner* of his death.

A few days later, I requested Watson to meet me at Baker Street. I had received the results of the post-mortem. Dr. Cronin kindly sent me the details in advance of the inquest. The immediate cause of cause of death was loss of blood. The blood was deoxygenated. There were no signs of heart disease. Yet lesions on the face acquired before death showed that he was not able to stop himself falling, as if he were smitten by a sudden paralysis.

Watson interjected to say this was not typical of a malaria faint. Ordinarily the victim would feel sick and dizzy and sit or lie down before the fever made him collapse.

Apart from the facial injuries there were some scratches on the hand, some recent bruising on the hip and a small puncture in the sole of the left foot. Suggestive, is it not.

I needed to re-examine the crime scene. Therefore, we made our return to the Anderson house. The widow did not seem best pleased at seeing us again. However, she passed us to Mr Doggett who conducted us to the terrarium. Once Doggett had left us, I dropped to the floor and began a thorough search of the area about the doorway.

At last! From behind the bench, I retrieved a small clump of two long and twisted thorns. Undoubtedly the tips themselves had been dipped in poison. It was a poison which causes loss of muscular control, but not death. To be specific, curare!

As it takes effect only through a cut, it is admirably suited for smearing on to arrowheads, or in this instance, a thorn. A bird will die in under a minute, a small mammal in ten minutes and a large creature such as a man in perhaps twenty minutes. Remember the dead frog. It is a common trick to test the potency by pricking a frog with a poisoned dart, then counting the number of hops it is able to make before succumbing. I believed the frog was used for such a test.

The clump was crushed in appearance. It was placed in one of Anderson's working boots. When he stood up, he drove the thorn deep into his foot. Recollect that the coroner's report mentioned the small puncture in the sole. Anderson extracted the thorn and discarded it as we have seen. A few minutes later, by which time he had reached the pool, paralysis would have overtaken Anderson. Then he fell, a helpless prey to the leeches. The poison would be undetectable.

I suspected Mrs Anderson of the execution of the murder. Only she or Doggett could know his habits so well as to set the trap. However, I was less certain that hers was the will behind it. I am inclined to think that Señor Gomez was the guiding mind, indeed who provided the means.

As for why, Watson, why else but for love? Why does a woman do anything but for love? It is clear that her tenderness for Anderson had faded over the years. She told us she yearns to return to her native country. Her husband was often away for months at a time. He is many years her senior. They have no children.

Then one day a young man from her own country pays a visit. He talks to her in her own language of the scenes of her homeland. She falls in love with him. They exchange confidences. She reveals that Anderson is a spy for the royalist cause. As a good diplomat he reports this to his superiors and receives the order to kill him. No doubt he offered her a powerful inducement to commit murder. Marriage and a new life in the country she loves.

From his point of view it would be an advantageous match. She is the daughter of a government official. She inherits all of Anderson's not-inconsiderable wealth.

The horror of curare poisoning is that the victim is awake and aware of what is happening until the loss of consciousness. Anderson would have felt the leeches feeding on him but have been unable to call out. A most unpleasant death.

And so we returned to the house and requested a private audience with the widow.

I understand, Mrs. Anderson, that you are affianced to Señor Gomez. You killed your husband through the use of curare. It is my business to know what other people do not know. No, madam, the police have not yet been informed. But I have evidence enough which will convince them of your guilt. I feel little sympathy for you. Am I right in thinking it was inspired by Señor Gomez?

The woman straightened her head in defiance. She would not have another blames for what she had done. She had long since lost any feelings of love for her husband. He was a traitor to her country, and therefore he deserved to die, she said. She wished to be free.

Gomez of course had the privilege of diplomatic immunity. I could hardly allow Mrs Anderson to be sentenced to hang whilst he went free. Therefore, I insisted that she and her lover leave England immediately. Their failure to do so would result in the official police force being informed of their crime.

Mrs Anderson went to speak, but I turned upon my heel and left the room, with Watson at my side. It was disappointing to see justice thwarted in this way. My only consolation was a firm belief that Mrs Anderson and Senor

Gomez would enjoy but little happiness together in the years to come. It was my duty of course to appraise Sir Joseph Dalton Hooker of my findings in the affair. However, the official verdict reached apropos the late Mr John Anderson's death, and the facts in the matter of his cold-blooded murder, would be separate matters entirely.

Don't Go Into The Cellar! Recordings

Theatre Recordings

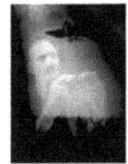

You can order recordings of many of our performances from our online shop -

https://cellartheatre.myshopify.com/

And learn more about us at -

Website – www.dontgointothecellar.com

About MX Publishing

MX Publishing is the world's largest specialist Sherlock Holmes publisher, with over four hundred titles and two hundred authors creating the latest in Sherlock Holmes fiction and non-fiction.

Our largest project is The MX Book of New Sherlock Holmes which is the world's largest collection of new Sherlock Holmes Stories – with over two hundred contributors including NY Times bestsellers Lee Child, Nicholas Meyer, Lindsay Faye and Kareem Abdul-Jabbar. The collection has raised over $85,000 for Stepping Stones School for children with learning disabilities.

Learn more at www.mxpublishing.com

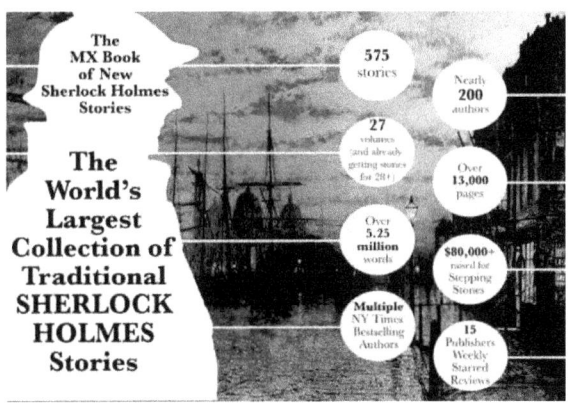

(as of May 2021 – more volumes on the way!)

www.ingramcontent.com/pod-product-compliance
Ingram Content Group UK Ltd.
Pitfield, Milton Keynes, MK11 3LW, UK
UKHW040847260326
469383UK00009B/76